FOR IAN AND VALERIE, FELLOW LA BABIES, AND FOREVER THE MOST PRECIOUS —FF

TEXT AND ART © 2022 BY CHRONICLE BOOKS LLC.
ALL RIGHTS RESERVED. NO PART OF THIS BOOK MAY BE REPRODUCED IN ANY FORM WITHOUT WRITTEN PERMISSION FROM THE PUBLISHER.

LIBRARY OF CONGRESS CATALOGING-IN-PUBLICATION DATA AVAILABLE.

ISBN 978-1-7972-0721-6

MANUFACTURED IN CHINA.

MIX
Paper from responsible sources
FSC
www.fsc.org
FSC™ C104723

TEXT BY FEATHER FLORES.
ILLUSTRATIONS BY ASIA ELLINGTON.
DESIGN BY MARIAM QURAISHI, ABBIE GOVEIA, AND SANDY FRANK.
TYPESET IN SACKERS GOTHIC.
THE ILLUSTRATIONS IN THIS BOOK WERE RENDERED DIGITALLY.

10 9 8 7 6 5 4 3 2 1

CHRONICLE BOOKS LLC
680 SECOND STREET
SAN FRANCISCO, CALIFORNIA 94107

CHRONICLE BOOKS—WE SEE THINGS DIFFERENTLY.
BECOME PART OF OUR COMMUNITY AT WWW.CHRONICLEKIDS.COM.

TODAY'S A **BRIGHT** AND **SUNNY** DAY!

COME ON, LET'S GO EXPLORE **LA**!

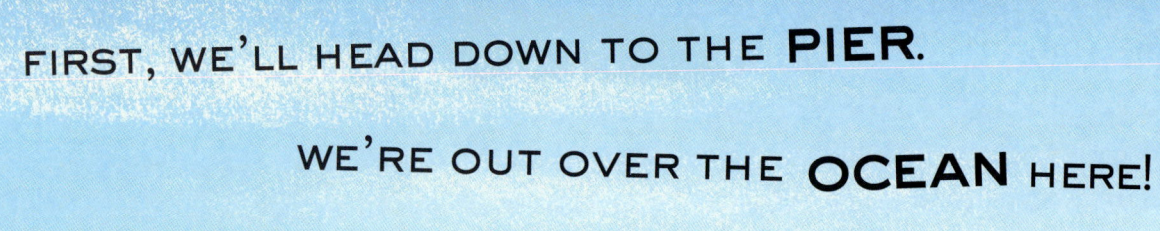

FIRST, WE'LL HEAD DOWN TO THE **PIER**.

WE'RE OUT OVER THE **OCEAN** HERE!

A **WOOLLY MAMMOTH!** DINOSAURS!
FEARSOME CATS WITH MIGHTY **ROARS!**

IF WE DREAM **BIG**, COULD WE FIND **OURS**?

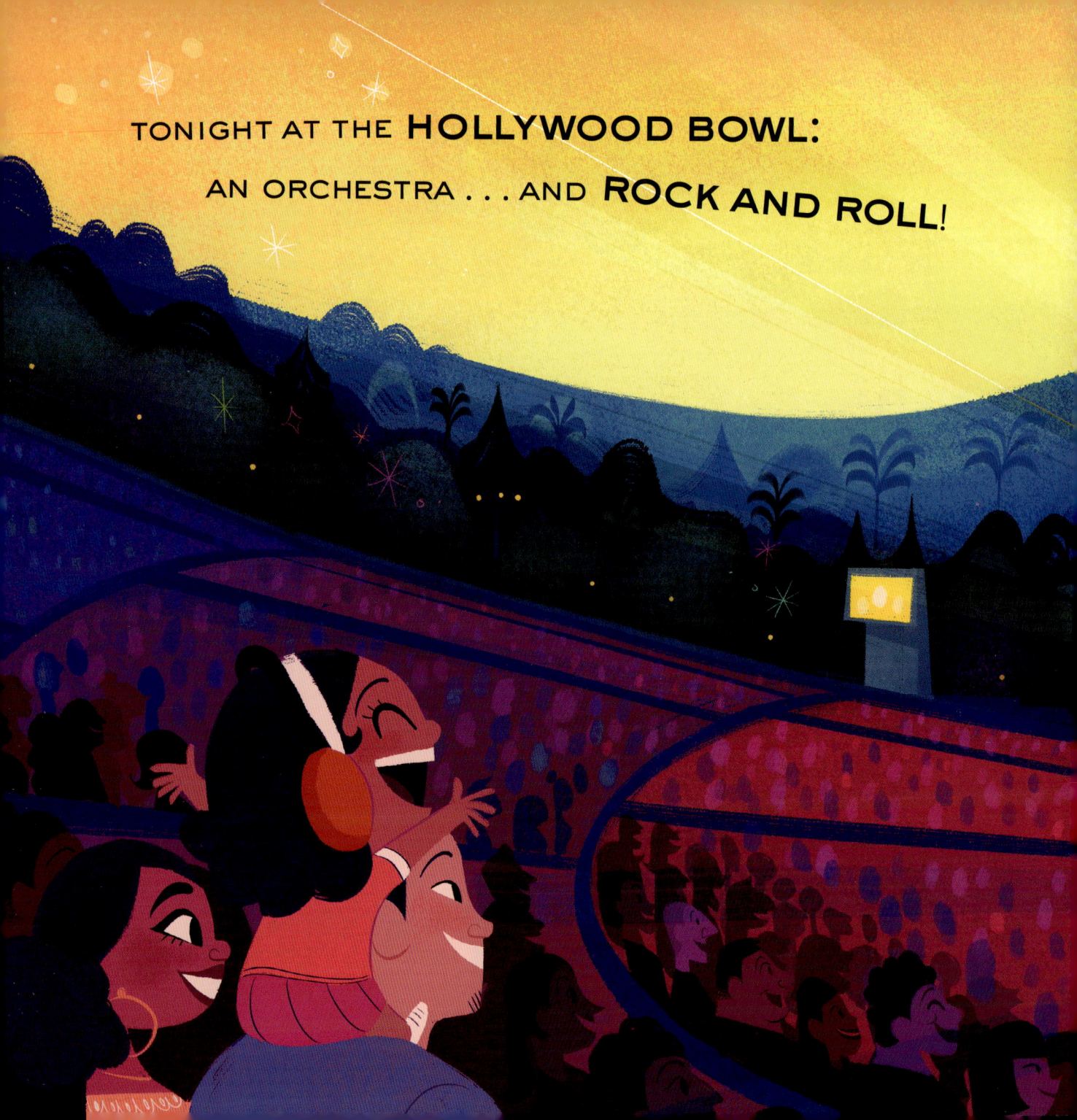